Riggs' Saviour

Kings Reapers MC - A Novella

Nicola Jane

Copyright © 2021 by Nicola Jane

All rights reserved.

No portion of this book may be reproduced in any form without written permission from the publisher or author, except as permitted by U.S. copyright law.

NOTE: Riggs' Saviour is a follow-up of Riggs' Ruin, but you will need to read the first four books in the Kings Reapers MC series to understand their story so far.

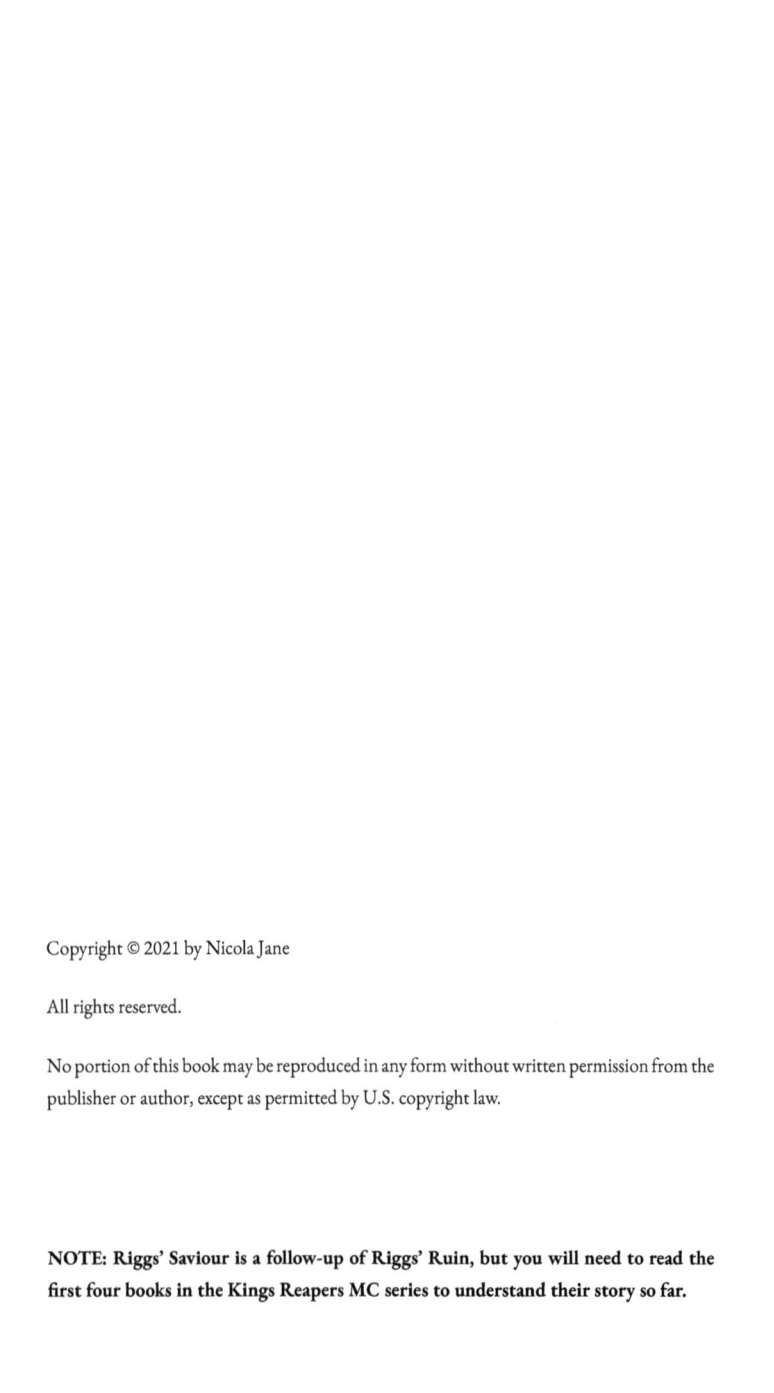

Meet the team

Cover Designer: Charli Childs, Cosmic Letterz Design
Editor: Rebecca Vazquez
Proofreader: Amanda Tabor
Formatting: Nicola Miller
Publisher: Nicola Jane

NOTE: Riggs' Saviour is a follow-up of Riggs' Ruin, but you will need to read the first four books in the Kings Reapers MC series to understand their story so far.

Disclaimer:

Names, Places, Situations in this book, are all from the imagination of the author, and any resemblence is purely coincidental.

Spelling Note:

Please note, this author resides in the United Kingdom and is using British English. Therefore, some words may be viewed as incorrect or spelled incorrectly, however, they are not.

Acknowledgements

It's been a long time coming, but I am so happy to finally bring you Riggs' Saviour. I felt Riggs needed to explain himself to all the readers who were so mad at his behaviour towards Anna, and just in general—let's face it, he's been an arse! I hope you forgive him.

Thank you for sticking with the Kings this far, it means the world xx

Trigger Warning

If you're easily offended, you might hate this story. Riggs is the club president, and he makes no apologies for behaving like an alpha-hole. He uses terrible language, makes many mistakes, and treats Anna terribly for a short while.

Any complaints should be directed his way...

Contents

PLAYLIST	VIII
CHAPTER ONE	1
CHAPTER TWO	9
CHAPTER THREE	13
CHAPTER FOUR	21
CHAPTER FIVE	33
CHAPTER SIX	41
CHAPTER SEVEN	51
CHAPTER EIGHT	61
CHAPTER NINE	69
CHAPTER TEN	73
CHAPTER ELEVEN	79
A note from me to you	82

PLAYLIST

Afterglow - Ed Sheeran

   Exile - Taylor Swift

   No Hard Feelings - Melii

   Can't Rely on You - Paloma Faith

   Say You Won't Let Go - Machine Gun Kelly ft. Camila Cabello (Cover Version)

   Someone You Loved - Camila Cabello (Cover Version)

   Take Care - Drake ft. Rihanna

   Don't Watch Me Cry - Jorja Smith

   You Mean the World to Me - Freya Ridings

   I Choose You - Kiana Ledé

   Tired Heart - Bmike ft. Nyx

   You broke me first - Tate McRae

   Monster - Shawn Mendes ft. Justin Bieber

   Some Say - Nea

   Surrender - Natalie Taylor

   Love the Way You Lie - Eminen ft. Rihanna

   Circles - Post Malone

Trust In You - Lauren Daigle
He Leaves You Cold - Passenger
Something to Remind You - Staind
At My Worst - Pink Sweats

CHAPTER ONE

ANNA

I glance at the clock beside my bed. Three a.m. Christ, I love my baby daughter, but I wish she'd sleep for more than an hour at a time. I get out of bed and go over to Willow's crib. I know she can't help it, she's suffering terribly with reflux, so I cuddle her to my chest and begin to walk around the room. The movement seems to calm her.

I stare at the space in my bed where my husband should be, and I sigh. As usual, it's empty. Things haven't been going well between us since I announced I was pregnant with Willow. We've spent a whole year of arguing, separating, making up, trying, but ultimately, we're not happy. Not like before.

That familiar pain fills my chest and tears brim in my eyes. I can't keep putting myself through this. Riggs thinks I tricked him into the pregnancy, but I didn't, and I'm so sick of repeating myself. Accidents happen, and so what? We're married and we already have a kid each, so I didn't think it was such a big deal. In fact, I thought he'd be over the moon. Turns out, I was so very wrong.

He loves Willow, I know he does. The fact he's not as hands-on as I expected doesn't bother me. After all, he's the president of the Kings Reapers MC, and lord knows he has a lot of club shit to deal with, but it hurts my heart that he's not as invested in her as he could be. And she adores him, oblivious to his lack of interest in her. Whether it's his voice or just the beating of his heart, whenever he cradles her, she's calm, and boy, could I do with a night of calm.

She begins to whimper again. I take her blanket from the crib and wrap her in it then make my way onto the landing. I creep across to Riggs' son's room. Sometimes he'll jump into bed with Ziggy so he doesn't wake us, but Ziggy is lying like a starfish, completely alone.

I check in on Malia, my six-year-old daughter. She's also deep in sleep.

I head downstairs. The clubhouse is silent for a change. Sometimes these guys can party all night, but it seems tonight is not one of those nights. I tap on Riggs' office door. "What?" he snaps.

I push it open and stick my head around the door. He's looking relaxed, lying on his office couch with a whiskey in his hand, and Raven sits at his desk. Her smile fades. "I was just checking you were okay," I say. "But I see I didn't need to worry."

"We're just talking," says Riggs, looking slightly irritated by my presence.

"At three a.m.," I note. "The time when everyone leaves their wife in bed and chats to other women."

"I'll leave you guys to it," says Raven awkwardly.

"No, you don't have to go," Riggs protests, sitting up.

"You really do," I say. I like Raven, she's friendly with all the guys and not in a way I feel threatened by, but still, he's my husband and it's three in the morning. As she gets level with me, I catch her eye. "Don't let me catch you sniffing around him, Raven. I'll kick your ass out of here if I think for one minute you're after him."

"Noted," says Raven stiffly as she leaves.

"Was that necessary?" asks Riggs.

"I don't know, was it?" I snap.

"I'm the club president. If I wanted a quick fuck, I'd choose a girl less likely to tell your girlfriends," he mutters.

"I'm trying, Finn," I say firmly. I only use his first name when I'm trying to break down his walls, though it never works these days. "But you gotta stop pushing me away. I can't keep fighting for us on my own. If you're not in this marriage anymore, then say it."

"You're always so dramatic, Anna," he says, sighing. "Fuck, I was chatting to a pretty girl at three a.m., shoot me. Some club presidents would have been doing a lot more than that!"

"Why are you trying to push me away?" I suddenly cry. He looks sad for a second before pulling himself together. "Something's wrong, I know it is. Why won't you talk to me?"

"It's easier to talk to everyone but you," he mumbles. My heart squeezes. "You don't listen. You think you do, but you're so distracted, and that's only when you're not moaning in my fucking ear."

His harsh words slay me. Nobody wants to be described as a nagging wife and I try my

hardest to avoid moaning at him, for that reason! "I'm making you unhappy." I say it more as a statement than a question.

He knocks back the last of his drink. "Go back to bed."

"Come with me," I say. I hate it that I sound so needy. Why do I beg like that? He

shakes his head. "Please, Riggs." His jaw clenches and he sighs before putting his glass on his desk. I feel a small satisfaction as he follows me upstairs to our room. I lay Willow, who has now settled, in her crib and climb into bed. Riggs strips down to his boxer shorts. He hasn't touched me in months. The most I get these days is a kiss on the head, like I'm a child.

I move closer to him, snuggling into his side. He eventually wraps an arm around me. "I love you," I whisper.

"I love you," he whispers back and I smile. It's these times that make me think we'll make it. If we have love, then surely we have hope.

I run my fingers over his ripped chest, slowly making my way downwards. I lean up slightly and lay kisses along his strong jaw until I reach his mouth. I've almost forgotten what it's like to kiss him properly. I sweep my tongue into his mouth and gently push my hand into his boxer shorts. He's soft. He's not even stirring down below. I nip back along his jaw and down his neck, across his chest, and down his stomach.

He takes my arm, stilling me. "Not tonight," he whispers.

I bite back the disappointment and nod, lying back down beside him. He kisses my cheek and rolls over, turning his back to me. A single tear escapes, rolling down my face. His rejection hurts more than his harsh words.

Willow wakes at four, then five, and when it gets to six, I give up and get out of bed. Riggs is awake, staring at the ceiling. "You want me to take her?" he asks.

"I'm awake now," I mutter, lifting her from her crib and wondering just how long he laid there listening to her before I woke. Knowing he could have let me get some sleep just pisses me off more. "I know Willow is still young, but I'm thinking of looking for a part-time job,"

I announce. Getting out of the club for a few hours is just what I need to take my mind off whatever's going on between us.

"You're right, she's too young," he mutters.

"She's already taking formula over breast milk," I say. "She'll be fine with Frankie and Esther, and they offered to help out." His mum, Frankie, was more than happy to help and my best friend's mum, Esther, also lives at the club and I see her like my own mum, so with the childcare covered, I'm all set. "My old job is free and Darren said he'd take me back anytime."

"Darren? The guy who fancies you?" he asks. "You have it all worked out."

"I think it'll do us good," I say quietly. "Give us a chance to miss each other." It's all excuses. He doesn't see me during the day anyway, and at the minute, he doesn't come to bed either.

"The answer is no," he mutters, throwing the sheets back and reaching for his jeans.

"I wasn't asking," I say under my breath, leaving the room.

Leia is in the kitchen feeding her newborn baby. "Morning," she smiles. She gave birth weeks ago and she's looking amazing. Motherhood suits her.

"How do you look so amazing at this hour?"

"Plenty of coffee," she says, grinning. "Plus, Chains did the night feeds."

"Lucky you," I mumble.

"Riggs not helping out?" she asks, her expression sympathetic.

"Not really." I try not to tell the girls the exact extent of our problems. They all have their own stuff going on, and honestly, even I'm sick of hearing myself talk about it. But Leia is Riggs' sister and I hate putting her in the middle, even though I consider her a good friend. "In other news, I might be going back to work."

"Really?" she asks. "I thought you'd stay at home with Willow."

I shrug. "I need to feel like me again. I love being a mum, but since Reggie, I have this continuous worry that I need to have my own money, just in case."

"In case of what?" she asks. "Riggs would never see you without, you know that, and it's not like you two are splitting up or anything," she says, laughing. When I don't laugh, her smile fades. "Anna?"

"I just need to get back to work. I asked my old boss for my cleaning job back and he said there's plenty of work."

"Wasn't he a bit of a creeper?" she asks. "Does Riggs know about all of this? I don't think he'll be keen on you scrubbing floors again."

"He'll be fine about it. I spoke to him this morning. He just needs time to get used to the idea."

She stares at me for a long second. "He'll be fine? About you working for that creeper? About you scrubbing floors?" she asks, and I nod. "Right, something's going on. Talk to me," she says firmly.

The kitchen door opens and Riggs walks in. We fall silent. "Anna wants to go back to work," Leia announces and I glare at her.

"I know," he mutters, switching on the coffee pot.

"And you're okay with it?" she asks.

He shrugs. "I already told her no but looks like she's made her mind up if she's talking to you about it."

"Her boss was weird. He fancied Anna and was constantly asking her out," she says.

"Leia, don't say it like it's so hard to believe. I was attractive back then," I say jokingly but with a hint of seriousness.

"That's not what I meant. You're very attractive," she snaps. "Isn't she, Riggs?" He nods and heads for the door. "Don't you care that another man wanted your wife even though she was pregnant at the time?" snaps Leia. "Imagine how he'll be now she isn't pregnant!"

"Christ, Leia, it's too early for this shit. Get off my back. If Anna wants to work, then who am I to stop her?"

He leaves the room and Leia stares wide-eyed at me. "Are you guys splitting up?"

I shrug because right now, I don't know.

CHAPTER TWO

ANNA

"As you can see, not much has changed," says Darren with a smile. It's been a week since I told Riggs about my job, and today is my first day. "The rest of the team are meeting for drinks at lunch. Join us. It'll be great for you to meet everyone."

"I have to get back," I say.

"One won't hurt," he says, patting my arm. I find myself agreeing.

I throw myself into cleaning the offices that Darren has been contracted out to deep clean. It feels good to concentrate on something other than the kids. Don't get me wrong, I love them all so much, including Ziggy, but with Riggs' lack of attention, I'm finding that they depend on me way more than him and I'm drained. So much so, I'd rather clean for someone than be at home. Ziggy and Malia are both in school during the day anyway and Riggs agreed to do the drop-off each morning if I'd do the pick-up. Between him, Frankie, and Esther, the kids will be just fine.

After my shift, I head for the bar that Darren told me about. It'll be nice to see some of my co-workers again and meet new faces. All of my friends are involved with the club, which is great, but sometimes I crave normal talk that doesn't involve gossip about club girls or which member came back covered in blood.

I spot Darren with a group of people. He introduces me to Maisey, Ella, and Cammie, who all seem lovely. One drink turns into two and then three, and when I eventually check the time, it's four o' clock. "Fuck, I have to go," I say, pulling out my phone.

I have three missed calls from Riggs. I'm surprised he even noticed I was gone. I'm about to call him back when the door opens and Blade saunters in. He smirks when he sees me. "Tut tut, you're in trouble," he sing-songs.

"I didn't see the time," I say. "I was just about to come home. Are the kids okay?"

"Yeah, fine. Esther picked Ziggy and Malia up and Willow's with Frankie. No harm done, although I don't think Riggs sees it like that."

Dread fills me. I know Riggs would never hurt me, but my past haunts me and it's hard to shake the fight or flight response when I know I'm about to face another argument.

Riggs is in his office, but I see him look over at me through the office window as I walk into the club. I head straight to Malia and Ziggy and give them each a kiss. "Sorry, Esther," I say. "I lost track of time."

"It's fine. When you didn't come home after lunch, I figured you'd gotten side-tracked."

I take Willow from Frankie. "Thanks, Frankie. Has she been okay?"

"Absolutely fine," says Frankie with a smile. "Take no notice of Riggs. I love having Willow."

"You planning on coming and apologising to me?" snaps Riggs from the doorway of his office.

"Apologise for what?" I ask, handing Willow back to Frankie. "Did you even bother to check in on Willow today?"

"Of course, I did, but I'm working too, yah know."

"I'm gonna take a shower," I say, turning to Frankie. "Are you okay with her for ten more minutes?"

"Of course, take your time."

I head for the stairs, but Riggs snatches my arm in his hand and I suck in a surprised breath. He releases me and we both stare at the spot where he grabbed me. "You can't just disappear like that," he says, trying to sound calmer than he is.

"I didn't disappear," I retort, rushing up the stairs with him hot on my ass.

"I tracked your phone. You were in a bar all afternoon,"

"Then you knew I hadn't disappeared," I snap. I head into the bathroom and turn on the shower. Riggs stands in the doorway, watching as I get undressed. "I went for a drink to meet the others. I lost track of time."

"You can't just go to the bar and forget you have kids," he mutters.

I glare at him. "I'd never forget about the kids. I love them all so much. It was a few drinks with my new co-workers and there are loads of adults in this place to help out with childcare, not to mention that you're Willow's dad and you've been here all day."

"This is how it starts," he snaps. "A harmless drink here and there, and before you know it, you're out all the time, drunk all the time, and I'm raising the kids on my own."

I place my hands on my hips. He doesn't look at my naked body like he used to and he certainly doesn't react how he once did. "When will you stop punishing me for Michelle's mistakes?" I demand to know. "She left Ziggy because she was an addict. I'm not! I'd never leave the kids. You checked out on me and the kids long ago. Just because you're still around, doesn't mean you're here."

"You can't just walk out on the kids when you feel like it. This is the reason I didn't want you to fucking work. You forgot about them on your first day!" he yells.

"I can't do this," I say, tears suddenly filling my eyes. "Oh god, I can't." The realisation hits me like a tonne weight and I pick my clothes up and begin to dress again.

"What are you talking about?" he asks, confusion on his face.

"This," I say, pointing back and forth between us. "It's too hard." I suck in a shaky breath and turn the shower off. I push past him and stand in the bedroom, wondering what to do first.

"What does that even mean?" he asks.

"It means I've got to get out of here," I say.

"And go where?"

"Anywhere," I say, grabbing a bag from the wardrobe. "I can't pretend that this is okay anymore."

"So you're leaving me?"

I stop and stare at him. "Yes," I confirm. "I'm leaving you."

CHAPTER THREE

ANNA

I haven't even left and I feel lighter. Riggs watches as I pack up some clothes for me and the girls. Leia walks in and stops when she sees me stuffing clothes into a bag. "What's going on?" she asks.

"I'm leaving," I say, adding a smile.

"What?" she screeches, glaring at Riggs. "And you're just gonna let her?"

"Maybe it's for the best," he mumbles. I try not to let his words break me. This is the right decision for me and my girls. "Besides, we've been here before, haven't we?" he asks, staring at me. "But you always come back."

I smile, though it doesn't reach my eyes. "But this is the first time I've felt happy to go, so what does that tell you?"

"No," says Leia. "No, it's not for the best. You haven't tried to save it," she says. "You could try counselling," she suggests. "And what about your job? Who will watch the kids when you go to work?"

I shrug. "I don't know. I haven't thought about that yet, but I know I have to leave. I can't stand living like this anymore."

"Where will you go?" she asks.

"I don't know," I say and laugh. This is all so sudden, but I feel relieved. "A hotel, maybe a bedsit somewhere. Just until I find something."

"You can't take Willow into a bedsit," wails Leia.

Riggs pulls out his wallet and takes out a stack of notes. He holds the bundle out and I stare at it. "Go to a hotel," he says. "I'll find a more permanent place for you by tomorrow."

I smirk at his offer and shake my head, not making a move to take his money. "You own half of everything," says Riggs. "Take the money."

I pick up my bag and stare him in the eyes. "No. I don't need it. I'll make my own way. I did it before and I'll do it again."

"I don't want the girls to go without," he snaps. "Now's not the time to be a martyr."

I stop, keeping my back to him. "That's what you think I'm trying to be?" I ask, slowly turning to face him. "I've spent my entire life fighting. For me, for my daughter, and now for both my girls. I thought you were the one. I'm not being a martyr by refusing your guilt money. I'm standing on my own two feet for once. I'm taking control of my life and I'm putting myself first. I'll be in touch about contact with Willow," I pause, "if you want contact, that is." "Of course I want contact with my daughter," he snaps.

I laugh but it's without humour. "She's been right under your roof all this time and you've hardly spent any time with her. Don't have contact because it's what you think you have to do."

"I love her," he mutters.

"It's just words, Finn," I mumble. "Empty words."

Riggs leaves. I'd like to think it's because he can't stand to watch me shove my life into bags but I think he just wants to be out of my way. I make quick work of packing up some toys and extra clothes for both girls. The door opens and Eva rushes in. "Is it true?"

I nod, unable to hold the tears back from my best friend. "I've been so miserable," I mutter. "I can't do it anymore."

"I'll come too," she says, taking my hand.

I shake my head. "No, Cree loves you. You belong here."

"But you'll be on your own," she whispers.

"It's time for me to stand on my own two feet. No more men," I say, forcing a smile. "I'm looking forward to the challenge."

We head downstairs, where Vinn's waiting. "Your chariot awaits, madam," he says to me. When it's clear I have no idea what he's talking about, he looks to Leia.

"I asked for his help," she explains. "He's got houses and stuff."

"You really don't need to," I say to Vinn, and he smiles fondly at Leia.

"You know I can't say no to her," he grins. Chains mutters something under his breath. He hates that the mafia kingpin has a soft spot for his ol' lady.

Riggs takes Willow from Frankie and carries her to his office, snuggling his face against her. It breaks my heart, but there's no way around it. I can't leave my girls here and I can't stay. I kiss Ziggy on the head. "I've gotta go away for a while," I say and he touches my hair. "I'll speak to Daddy about him letting you stay with us on the weekends and coming for dinner a few nights in the week?" He nods. It isn't the first time Riggs and I have taken a break, so sadly, he's used to this, but seeing the sorrow in his eyes hurts my heart. I question myself for the hundredth time, but I know deep down this is the right thing to do.

I wait a few minutes, then go to the office. "We're leaving," I say softly. Riggs nods, walking towards me with his face still close to

Willow. "I'll text you the address and we'll sort out contact. I'd still really like to see Ziggy and I know he'd like to see Willow and Malia."

"This doesn't feel right," he whispers. "I don't know what to do to fix it." For the first time, I see the lost boy look in his eyes and I hesitate. He wants to talk. I wait a few seconds, but he doesn't continue, and I lose hope.

I take Willow from him. "It's not because I don't love you," I say, quietly. "It's because I love you too much. I can't stay around while we destroy each other. My heart can't take it."

Vinn hands me the keys as I stand in the living room, looking around in awe. This place is amazing and situated ten minutes from the clubhouse. "Are you sure?" I ask.

"Yeah. It was standing empty. It may as well go to some use."

"What sort of rent are you looking for?" I ask warily, knowing this place is out of my price range.

"You're Riggs' ol' lady. This place is rent-free for you."

I shake my head. "No, I'll pay."

"If anyone is gonna pay, it'll be him. I'm not taking money from you."

"Vinn, I've left Riggs. He can't pay my rent," I say, laughing. "The whole point is to get my independence back."

"Get back on your feet and we'll discuss it."

I watch him leave and lock the door behind him, then I let out a breath. This morning, I had no idea this is where I'd end up.

I call my boss and explain my situation. Without childcare, I can't work, and I don't want to keep running to the club for help. I want Riggs to see I can stand on my own two feet, and who knows, maybe I'll learn to be strong again. To get me through financially, I have an account that my ex set up. It's got more than enough money in it, but so far, I haven't touched it. The idea was I'd save it for Malia, but this is an emergency and I'll work hard to pay every penny back once I'm back on my feet.

I'm making dinner when there's a knock at the door. Cree greets me with a smile. "Riggs asked me to bring Willow's crib," he says. It's a nice thing to do, but it sends a stab to my heart.

"Great," I say, forcing a smile. He goes back to his van, returns with the crib, and I take it. It's a travel one, so it pops up easily. "Is he okay?" I ask quietly.

"You know Riggs," he mutters. "He's locked away in his office."

"Look after him for me, Cree."

"This ain't forever, Anna," he says and I smile.

It is.

RIGGS

It was the perfect time to tell her. I could have said the words and it would have explained everything. They were on the tip of my tongue and then she shut me down, and who can blame her? I've fucked up so bad, even I don't wanna talk to me. I stare at my phone, willing it to ring. I'd got Willow's crib and was stepping out of the club to take it myself, but then Eva stopped me, telling me to give Anna space. *Space.* That one little word means so much.

Cree enters the office without an invite and flops onto the chair opposite me. "Well, what a clusterfuck."

"Helpful," I mutter. "Are they your words of wisdom for the day?"

"I sat back when Michelle screwed you over. I hated that bitch and I was glad she fucking left. My only regret is not being honest with you back then and telling you what a blood sucking leech she really was. But Anna is—"

"Gone," I snap, cutting his words off. "I don't need to hear how fucking amazing she is, brother. I know all that shit. But she's gone, just like Michelle went. The only blessing is, she'll take care of my kid and I ain't gotta lose sleep wondering if Willow is okay."

"I don't get it," he utters.

"You don't need to. What happened to you hating talking about feelings and shit? Stick to what you're good at, brother. Be my VP, not my fucking counsellor."

"Shit, Pres. Ain't that what I'm doing right now? Being your VP. That's why I'm here feeling uncomfortable and shit. Telling you you're an arse. Letting her go is your biggest mistake yet, and trust me, you've made a few of those just lately."

"What the hell's that supposed to mean?" I yell.

Cree stands and heads for the door. "Take a look at yourself. This place is falling to shit and you lock yourself away in here. That's your answer. You're not leading this club right now, Riggs."

"Are you shitting me?" I growl. "I cleared the deal with Vinn and Blu."

"That was all Blu's doing, Pres. Without him, we would have lost the shipments and you know it. You gotta sort your shit out." He heads back towards the desk and places a business card down. He slides it towards me. "Call her. You told me she'd sort me out and she did. Now, it's your turn to get some help cos I don't know what the hell is going on with you, but shit's gotta change."

I let him leave before picking up the business card. It brings a smile to my face. "What an arse," I mutter, out loud.

I stare up at the building before me. It's not how I pictured a place like this. I press the buzzer and a female voice asks me how she can help. I snigger, because she can't help me, but for the good of the club, I've agreed to this bullshit. "Finn James to see Eleanor Chapman."

The door clicks open and I go inside, taking a seat in a small waiting area where the receptionist clicks away at speed on her computer keyboard. Eventually, a side door opens and a female steps out. She's stunning. Long, wavy dark hair, a pencil skirt with a white blouse tucked inside, and thick-rimmed glasses perched on her nose. Fuck, she looks like something out of a porn film. Funny that Cree never mentioned that part.

"Finn," she smiles warmly. "Come in."

Inside, the room is exactly what I pictured—a posh-looking couch by a bookcase and a comfy chair next to it. I smirk and shake my head at the irony. "Something amuse you?" she asks with a smile. She takes a seat in the comfy chair and points to the posh couch.

"It's all very," I wave my hand around the room, "cliché"

She smiles again, looking around the room. "I guess it is. So, tell me what brings you here."

I sit on a stool because I don't wanna get too comfy. I don't plan to be here long cos honestly, what the hell is this woman gonna do to make me sort my life out? Unless she can work a miracle.

"My brother is a client of yours. He told me to come."

"Let me guess," she says. "Elijah?" I nod. "I recognised the badges," she says, pointing her pen at my kutte.

"Seems to think you helped him, but I remember the arguments I had cos he didn't think he needed you. Only, he had to come to meet terms set out by the courthouse."

She nods in agreement. "I gave him a very good report. He finished his probation."

"But he still sees you," I state.

"Umm, you know I can't tell you things like that," she says. "Why did Elijah tell you to come and see me?"

"He thinks I'm having some kind of breakdown," I mutter.

"Do you think that?" she asks, and I shake my head. "But you still came here," she says thoughtfully.

"I need to get Cree off my back. He's upset because me and Anna have split."

"Anna's your?" she asks.

"Wife."

"Married for how long?" she asks.

"Not long enough," I mutter.

"You didn't want to break up?" she asks.

I take a minute to think about it. "I don't know what I want anymore. Loving Anna makes me weak. I can't lead the club when I'm weak."

"Yet you love her anyway, even though you broke up."

"But that'll stop. One day. Love doesn't last forever."

CHAPTER FOUR

ANNA

I look over the paperwork and smile as I sign my name on the dotted line then hand it to the tutor. "I think online learning is the best idea. You can work it around your life, kids, and work. I'm here anytime you need anything. Just email me at this address." She hands me a card and I tuck it inside my bag.

As I leave the college building, I feel a flicker of hope. *This is a new beginning. I can do this!* I'm busy texting while I walk, so I don't see him until I almost crash against his hard chest. "Anna," says Riggs. His voice still sends shivers throughout my body. I suck in a breath and stare up into his light blue eyes. Everything about this man makes me weak. "Where are the kids?"

"School, and Eva has Willow."

He nods. "You look nice." I'm thankful I made an effort for this meeting. I wanted the college to see me as determined and focussed rather than a crazy-haired mummy. I chose the tight-fitting jeans because it's the first time I've been able to squeeze into them since I'd gotten pregnant with Willow. I teamed them with a strappy top and leather jacket. Call me a sucker, but the smell of leather keeps me grounded. Eva did my hair this morning when she came over first thing to make sure I was dressed right for the meeting. She was more nervous than me. She'd given me a trim and cut bangs, saying they framed my face. "I like your hair like that," he adds.

"How's Ziggy?" I ask, because I can't listen to him say those nice things without wanting to cling to him.

"Missing you. I said I'd call about him coming to see you."

"I'll have him whenever is good with you. I miss him too."

I look behind Riggs to the old building he'd just exited. On the call buttons, the name Eleanor Chapman is highlighted. A stab of jealousy hits me, followed by fear. What if she's a solicitor? What if he's been to see her about a divorce?

"Are the girls okay?" he asks.

I nod. I hate this small talk. If he wants to divorce me, why won't he just say it? I feel my eyes water and I blink quickly. "I'm doing a course," I blurt out, mainly just trying desperately to fill the awkward silence. "Management."

He raises an eyebrow. "Like college?"

I nod. "Eva's idea. I always wanted to go back to college, but life seemed to get in the way. Reggie wouldn't let me . . ." I trail off. I haven't spoken about Reggie for such a long time.

"I'm nothing like him, Anna. If you wanted to go to college, you could have gone," he snaps. *Why does every conversation feel like an argument?*

"We never laugh anymore," I say, absentmindedly. "When did we stop laughing?"

"You never said you wanted to go to college," he mutters.

"I forgot. I was swept up in the kids and being a good wife. I guess I messed that up," I say, adding a small laugh.

"You didn't . . . mess it up, I mean."

"Then why are we behaving like we hardly know each other? Scared to say the wrong thing?" I take a deep breath. "I've deleted your phone number." He frowns but doesn't ask why. Maybe it's obvious. "I don't want to break down after a glass of wine and call you. I have a moment at least five zillion times a day where I think 'I should tell Riggs about this' and then I remember, I can't do that."

"You can," he says. "Anytime."

"I can't. Not if we're serious about this. I'm too weak for you. Anyway, when you want Willow, you'll have to call me."

"What if there's an emergency?" he asks.

"I'll call someone at the club," I say.

"What if you're in danger?" he adds.

I smile. "I'll call the cops. That's what normal people do, right?"

"Anna, you know what I mean. What if you're targeted because of your connection to the club?"

"I'll call Vinn."

Riggs scoffs. "Good old Vinn. Saved the day with a place to live and on call if you need him."

"He's doing it for Leia, not me. He respects you. Do you want my address?" I add.

He smirks. "You think you could take my kid without me knowing exactly where you are?"

I smile too. "I'd better go. Eva's waiting to hear news about my course."

He nods. "You want a lift home?"

I shake my head. Being on his bike, so close to him, it's too much too soon. "Bye," I mutter. I hold a breath as I walk away because I don't want to break down in the street. It's the longest we've spoken in months without having a blazing row. *Progress, right?*

Days turn to weeks and I throw myself into college work. I love it. I have a set routine of getting the kids bathed and in bed, then I pull out my laptop and get sucked into coursework. It's keeping my mind occupied.

But tonight, Riggs has Willow and Malia. I glance at the clock. He's due to return them in an hour. I haven't seen Riggs since meeting him in the street unexpectedly four weeks ago. Usually, he sends someone to collect the girls and drop them off. Same arrangement when I have Ziggy.

I shower and slip into my pyjama shorts and vest. I decide to get some work in before they arrive home and the bedtime routine starts.

I'm so lost in work that the knock on the door surprises me. I grab a hair tie and begin piling my hair on the top of my head, opening the door to Riggs with a child in each arm. My mouth opens and closes in surprise. I was expecting one of the Kings Reapers to drop them home. His eyes run up and down my body and I suddenly feel over-exposed. I know that hungry look in his eyes, even though it's been a while since he's directed it at me. I finish tying my hair and fold my arms across my chest.

"Did Malia eat her dinner?" I ask, weakly.

"You hiding something, Anna?" he asks, his voice rumbling through every part of my body.

"No," I almost whisper.

"You look surprised to see me. Are you gonna invite me in?"

I glance back over my shoulder at the laptop and workbooks all over the living room floor. Before I can answer, he steps forward, and I'm pushed against the wall as he brushes past me. "You hiding someone in here?" he asks.

I laugh, like I have time for anyone right now. "No. I was in the middle of working," I say, sighing.

He lets his eyes wander over the books. "You need a desk," he mutters.

"If that's all, I have baths and bedtime to be getting on with."

"You're working. I'll do it." I stare after him with confusion as he makes his way upstairs, still holding a child in each arm. I shrug. Not wanting to look a gift horse in the mouth, I sit back down amongst the books and continue to work.

An hour later, Riggs reappears. "All done."

I look up at him and smile. "Thanks. That was a huge help."

"You had some dinner?" he asks.

I shake my head, the reminder of lack of food making my stomach rumble loudly. I cover it with my hand and laugh. "I forgot."

"You always forget to eat?" he asks. "You've lost too much weight."

"I needed to drop a dress size," I say.

He scowls and marches towards the kitchen. "Who told you that crap?"

"I dunno," I mutter. "I guess . . . I mean, I thought . . ." I follow him and watch as he opens the fridge.

"You thought what?" he asks.

"That you didn't . . . erm . . . fancy me anymore." My cheeks burn with embarrassment at my confession.

He slams the fridge closed and turns to face me. "I never said that!"

"I know. We just stopped . . . yah know."

He looks hurt and reaches out, taking my hand. He tugs me towards him, and my heart almost beats out of my chest when his hand gently strokes along my jaw. "Baby, I never stopped fancying you."

"It doesn't matter now," I say, offering a small smile. Every touch sparks something deep within me, and he continues to stare into my eyes while stroking his thumb over my cheek. His mouth crashes against mine, and for a second, I freeze before melting against him and letting him thrust his tongue against my own in a hungry kiss. Fuck, I missed this. His hands move to my waist, then my ass. He pulls me against him and I feel his arousal pressing against my hip. He lifts me onto the worktop and his mouth descends along my neck then my shoulder. He gently tugs the strap of my vest until it falls down, exposing my breast to his hungry mouth. I throw my head back in pleasure as his tongue works magic. It's been so long since he's touched me, I'm on the brink of having an orgasm.

A banging from somewhere interrupts us. We both still, the sound of our heavy breathing filling the room. "The door," he mutters.

"Shit," I whisper, pulling the strap back into place. The banging comes again, but this time, it's louder. I jump with fright. Everything around me fades away, disappearing as I sit up with a start. Looking around, I'm lying on the living room floor, surrounded by my books.

"Fuck, Anna, are you in?" yells Riggs. I jump up and rush for the door. I rip it open and Riggs glares at me angrily. "I've been knocking on the door for ages," he snaps. He pushes past me and places Willow's car seat down on the floor. Malia skips in behind Riggs, happily singing to herself. "Why do you look flushed?" he snaps.

I rub my cheeks. "I just woke up," I mutter. "I must have nodded off while I was working."

"Enjoyed a nice nap, did you? Meanwhile, I'm looking after the kids so you can study."

I roll my eyes and unfasten Willow from the seat. "Willow wakes up a lot through the night. And don't act like you're doing me a favour. You wanted the girls tonight."

"How's all that going?" he asks, pointing to the books on the floor.

"Good," I say. "I'm enjoying it."

"I bathed the kids already. You want me to put them to bed so you can finish up your work?" he asks.

I smirk, the memory of my dream invading my mind. "I can do it," I say.

"Have you eaten?"

I shake my head, my cheeks reddening again. "Not yet."

"You go put them to bed and I'll get you a sandwich. I need to talk to you."

RIGGS

I haven't seen Anna for weeks. She looks fucking hot. The lack of sex in my life is not helping shit. I focus on making her a sandwich. When she returns, she's still got that damn flush on her cheeks. She only ever got that after an orgasm or if she was thinking naughty shit. I frown. "Did you have a guy here tonight?"

"No," she says, innocently.

"You took ages to answer the door. You got that 'just fucked' look. Shit, have you met someone?"

She rolls her eyes for the second time tonight and I have a few thoughts of my own. "What did you want to talk to me about?" she asks.

I place the sandwich down in front of her. "Eat, you've lost way too much weight," I mutter.

She almost chokes on the bread. "Drink," she pants, between coughs. I get her some water and she takes it gratefully.

"I've been to see a counsellor," I say, and her eyes widen. "She wants to meet you," I add.

"Why?" asks Anna.

"I don't know, Anna. Maybe she thinks she can work her voodoo shit and repair us." I've seen Eleanor twice now and she's good. I always go in there with the mindset that I ain't talking about Anna or any other shit that's going on, but somehow, I end up on that damn posh couch blurting out my life story. Now, she wants Anna to come.

"I don't know," mutters Anna, hesitantly. "I'm finally not crying anymore. I get into bed, read my book, and think about you for just a minute or two, and then I sleep. I don't cry like I used to. I don't allow myself to think about you long enough. Talking to a counsellor might make me cry again, and honestly, I have nothing left."

I nod stiffly. I told Eleanor I'd try, but I ain't begging. "Right. We need to sort out what happens next," I mutter. She waits for me to explain. "Well, we're apart. The next step is divorce," I say bluntly. I hadn't even thought about fucking divorce but I've said the words now and she looks like a fucking wounded puppy dog. My heart aches. "Shall I get the ball rolling?" I add, inwardly yelling at my stupid ass to shut the hell up, but I reason if she don't wanna see a counsellor, then she don't want us to work.

"Erm . . . yes, I guess."

"It's time to move forward," I mutter.

"Like meeting other people?" she asks quietly.

I nod. "Yeah. I got blue balls waiting around, and if we're done, then I can sort that

problem out." I laugh awkwardly and she frowns. "I don't want a relationship or anything, I'll use a clubwhore or . . ." I trail off. *What the fuck am I saying? Stop talking, asshole. Just stop.* "Raven."

She sucks in a breath and her eyes get that glazed look. "Raven," she repeats.

I stand stiffly, unsure how to get out of this ridiculous conversation. No wonder she fucking hates me. "We're not serious or anything," I say, shrugging. Christ, Raven isn't even on my radar, I'm using her cos of the way Anna reacted at finding us together in my office.

Anna pushes the sandwich away. "Baby, eat. Please," I say quietly. She's practically bones as it is and I wonder if that's my fault.

"I need you to go," she croaks, trying hard to keep her voice steady.

"Look, I shouldn't have said that," I say quickly.

She blinks and tears roll down her cheeks as she gives a watery smile. "I just remembered I have a phone call to make. Am I still having Ziggy tomorrow?" she asks. I nod. *I feel so ashamed.* "Great. I'll get him from school with Malia then."

I hook my finger around hers and she stares down at the connection with such pain on her face that I almost crack and tell her everything, because surely the truth is easier to handle than what I'm doing to her right now. "Anna," I mumble.

"I'm okay," she lies. "I'm gonna be okay."

I nod. "I know. You're strong." I gently kiss her forehead and she closes her eyes, pressing herself against me. The heat from her stirs something and I breathe in her strawberry shampoo scent. Fuck, I miss her. I place a finger under her chin and tilt her head back so she's looking into my eyes. I try desperately to convey how I feel through that look. She steps up onto her tiptoes and moves her mouth closer. She's so close, I feel the heat from her lips. That flush appears on her cheeks and I slam my mouth against hers. I'm so lost in her that it takes a second to register her fists hitting against my chest.

We pull apart. "No," she breathes, glaring at me. She swipes the back of her hand over her mouth. "You need to go now. Don't stand there telling me you want to fuck other women then kiss me like that," she hisses.

"I don't wanna fuck other women," I mutter.

"Get out, Riggs. You give me whiplash with your fucking moods."

The clubhouse is busy. Cree slaps me on the back. "You sort shit with Anna?"

I shake my head. "Why would I? We're over, remember?" I snap.

"She didn't wanna go and see Eleanor?" he guesses. I shake my head. "Sorry, man," he mutters.

"So I told her I was fucking Raven," I mutter, and Cree groans. "I know! When I said the fucking words, I wanted to rip my own throat out."

"Go back and tell her the truth," he says.

I shake my head. "Nah, it's done. She's done. What's the point? I gotta face it, Anna's moved on from me. I don't blame her. I'm an ass."

"It sounds to me like Anna doesn't want to come because she's guarding her heart. Not because she doesn't want to try," says Eleanor.

"It's the same fucking thing," I mutter, scrubbing my hands over my face. "She ain't here."

"Last time we talked about your past, with Michelle. Let's talk about your relationship with Anna."

I groan. "I think you enjoy watching me squirm," I mutter. "I don't cry. You ain't gonna make me cry."

Eleanor laughs. "There's nothing wrong with crying, Finn. Lots of people do it, it isn't a sign of weakness."

I scoff. "In my world, it is."

"Was Anna from your world?" she asks.

I shake my head. "Not really. Her last guy was a crime boss, so she wasn't clueless to our world, but she wasn't in it. He was violent to her. A lot."

"That must have been hard for her."

I nod. "But she's strong," I say, my words from last night slipping out.

"What makes someone strong?" she asks, and I frown in confusion. "Well, you say she's strong. But how do you know?"

I shrug. "She just is," I mutter. "She carried on, after he did shit to her. She left and carried on. She looked after their kid. And now, I've hurt her and she's carrying on, looking after my kid and his ... alone." I shake my head, hating that thought.

"She hasn't had a choice but to carry on," says Eleanor.

"No," I mutter.

"So you got together, you had a child. How was that?"

"Willow was ... unexpected," I say.

"A good surprise or bad?" she asks.

I pause. "I wasn't ready for another kid."

"But you already had Ziggy," she says. "What was the problem with having another?"

"Fuck, now you sound like her," I mumble. I stand and walk over to the window. "Anna wanted another kid. I told her no. I wanted to wait."

"For what?"

I shrug. "I don't know. I just wanted her," I snap. "I didn't have her to myself for long enough."

"You were jealous that the baby would have her attention?" she asks.

"Maybe," I mumble.

"It's a normal reaction," says Eleanor. "Lots of men feel like that when their partners get pregnant."

"She was so happy. I remember her announcing it to the club and she was smiling. It felt like she'd punched me when she said the words. And I thought to myself, if I feel like that, maybe none of it was right."

"None of it?" she repeats.

"Like us, the relationship. I questioned us. Then when she saw I wasn't happy and she gave me those puppy dog eyes, I lost my shit. Accused her of tricking me."

"Into getting pregnant?"

I nod, hanging my head. "I said I couldn't trust her if she'd tricked me into getting her pregnant just to keep me."

"Do you believe that?" she asks.

I shake my head and stare out at the London skyline. "No. She ain't like that."

"Did you feel that way when Michelle got pregnant?" she asks.

I nod slowly. "Yeah. But I was young and I was scared, so I pretended to be happy. Michelle did trick me. She admitted it one night when she was high."

"But with Anna, you were married. You each had a child. If she'd wanted to trap you, wouldn't she get pregnant before the wedding? Seems a strange time to get pregnant, in fact, it's the way most people do it—marriage, then babies."

"The thing is," I say, turning to face her, "a few hours before that moment, before she announced the news, I'd had some news of my own."

CHAPTER FIVE

ANNA

"Malia, please, just walk." I'm aware that I'm begging, but she's acting up so much lately that I'm losing my mind.

"My legs hurt," she wails. I sigh heavily and Ziggy slips his hand into my own.

"You want me to deal with her?" he asks. I smile down at him and nod. "Leave it with me." He adds a wink and I see Riggs in him, which makes me smile wider.

I watch him take Malia by the hand. "I'll help you walk," he says, smiling big to show off his dimples. Malia melts into a puddle and begins to walk.

Eva is inside my house cooking when we get home from the school run, and it reminds me of how things were before Riggs. Willow is sleeping soundly in her basket in the living room.

"You stinky little humans, go wash your hands before you eat," says Eva. The kids rush off upstairs and I take a seat at the table.

"Riggs wants a divorce," I blurt, and Eva freezes mid pouring of water from the vegetable pan.

"What?"

"He brought the girls home last night. I was so unprepared that I cried. I feel like such an idiot," I mutter. "I've managed not to break down, and as soon as he says that, I crumble like a fucking broken-hearted teenager."

"Shit, Anna, I'm so sorry."

"Don't be. It's the next step. He just caught me off-guard. I'd woken from a crazy dream about me and him and it was on my mind when he announced that."

"Crazy dream?" she asks, wiggling her eyebrows.

"Is Raven seeing anyone?" I ask, changing the subject.

"Not as far as I know. She lies pretty low these days. I'm so busy helping Leia with Hope that I haven't taken notice. Gia and Blu are the hottest news around the club. They've been married for months now, but they're all over each other. Were Cree and I that bad?" she asks. I smile and nod as she rolls her eyes. "Well, please accept my apology for my disgusting display of public affection. I'm embarrassed just thinking about it."

"Newlyweds are supposed to be disgustingly in love."

"Sorry," says Eva, with a groan. "You don't wanna be talking about this."

"It's fine. Riggs said he was seeing Raven, or fucking her, I'm not sure which."

Eva gasps. "No way. No fucking way. I'll ask Leia, Chains would have told her," she says.

I shake my head. "No. I don't want him to think I'm checking up on him. I'll be fine. I've got my kids and college. Things will work out. Besides, he can't stay single forever, can he? It was just sooner than I expected, and then I tortured myself all night wondering if they'd been together for ages, behind my back even. I told you she was in his office in the early hours that time."

"I hate the way he's been treating you. And it makes no sense, he went from being obsessed with you to behaving like he hates you!"

"One day, my prince will come," I say, laughing. We used to use that line a lot when we were younger. "But until then, I don't need a man."

At seven o'clock prompt, there's a knock. Riggs fills the doorway. Eva takes Ziggy to the car, eyeing Riggs as she passes him. "What's up with her?" he asks, and I shrug.

"Can I pop my head in to see Willow?" he asks. I nod, opening the door wider for him to step inside. Willow smiles when she spots him, wriggling her legs and making her bouncer wobble. He picks her up and smothers her in kisses.

"Did you get an appointment to see a solicitor?" I ask casually and he stares at me blankly. "About a divorce," I prompt.

"No, not yet. We should talk and decide how we're gonna do shit," he says.

"Get the papers drawn up and I'll sign. There's nothing to discuss."

"We gotta talk money, Anna."

I shake my head. "I don't need anything from you. I won't take you to the cleaners. Just pay towards Willow."

"You're entitled to half of everything I own," he mutters.

"I don't want it. I don't want anything," I say.

"You say that now because you're angry, but down the line, you'll need money for your future."

"That's why I'm at college, to better my future for me and the kids. I'm looking for a job. I can pay my own way. I've dipped into the money Reggie left in my account."

Riggs glares at me. "You used Reggie's money rather than asking me?"

"Technically, it's my money. It's wasted just sitting in the account, and besides, I'm raising his daughter. He should pay."

"I can give you money. I can provide for my wife and kid," snaps Riggs.

"I never said you couldn't. We're going around in circles. Anyway, we're separated. You don't need to pay for me anymore."

"We're still married," he sighs.

"Hopefully not for much longer," I say, adding a sarcastic smile.

Leia waits for me to reach her before wrapping me in her arms. "I miss you so

much," she cries.

"You're so dramatic."

She called me to meet for coffee. We find a table and take a seat, then a waitress takes our order. "I have something so exciting to ask you," she says, practically jumping up and down in her seat. "Vinn's opening a microbar," she says. "He needs a manager."

"Okay," I say, confused as to why this is so exciting.

"He wants you, Anna. He wants you to run it."

My eyes widen. "Really?"

"Yes!" she says, grinning. "It's a great little place on Queen's Road. You'll fall in love with it. He's done an amazing job on the place. Mum and Esther said they'd help with the kids when you need it, and of course, you have me, Eva, and anyone else who wants to help."

"I don't know what to say."

"Say yes!" she laughs.

"Yes! A hundred times yes!"

"Have you spoken to Riggs?" she asks, her smile fading.

"A little. He's talking divorce and splitting money," I mutter. "It's all a bit real."

"He's really sad. Locks himself away in his office all the time. Chains is worried, said he's never seen Riggs so crazy. He's making snappy decisions and getting his hands dirty instead of asking the brothers. It ain't like him."

"He told me he's sleeping with Raven," I say, and her eyes bug out of her head.

"Chains hasn't mentioned it and we all know he and Raven are as thick as thieves. Maybe Riggs is trying to make you jealous?" she suggests. I shake my head. If he's saying stuff like that, then he's thinking about doing it. "He's seeing a counsellor," she adds quietly. "Mum wasn't meant to tell me, but you know what she's like. It's clearly not helping if he's talking about divorce. We thought it'd help."

"Well, maybe it is. Maybe it's what he wants deep down and the counsellor made him see that."

"No," says Leia. "He loves you. He does. Something's happened to make him like this. We just have to figure it out."

RIGGS

I wait for my brothers to file into the room. Slamming the gavel onto the table, I finally get their attention. "Vinn has a shipment coming in tonight. I need you guys on the ball. No wandering off for a piss," I say, my eyes falling to the prospect. "No clowning around. This needs to be unloaded and reloaded in quick time."

"What we dealing with, Pres?" asks Brick.

"Glocks. But triple what we usually shift," I say.

"We expecting a war?" asks Blade, laughing.

"Who the fuck knows. All I know is Vinn has already sold over half the cases. We're gonna make some good money on this provided we can keep to our end of the deal." I turn to Brick. "Any news, treasurer?"

He shrugs, opening a large book. Most shit's done on the computer these days, but Brick prefers to write it down old school. "We made good figures this last month, Pres. We keep this up and dreams of turning the club around are a real possibility."

"Speaking of turning things around, we got the keys to the microbar yesterday. I have a manager lined up and bar staff. I'll be running the doors for the first few weeks," I say.

"You?" asks Blu.

"Yeah, me, brother. Problem?"

He shakes his head, smirking over at Cree. "Usually you pass that shit to us."

"Well, I don't wanna risk you fuckers screwing up the first clean business we've owned. I don't want it getting back to Anna that we own this place either. As far as she's concerned, It's Vinn's."

I arrive five minutes early for my appointment with Eleanor. Her receptionist smiles at me in the hungry way she does every time I sit in the waiting room. "This is so unprofessional of me," she begins, "but I was wondering if you're single?"

"It's complicated," I mutter.

"I know all about complicated," she says, rolling her eyes. "Maybe we can hook up for a drink some time and compare stories?"

I stare at her for a minute. She's pretty, blue eyes, blonde hair, good sized tits, and a feistiness about her, but I find myself shaking my head. "You're right," I say as the office door opens and I stand. "It's very unprofessional of you."

Eleanor takes her usual seat. "How's things?" she asks.

"I fucked things up with Anna, even more than before," I say bitterly. "I said a load of shit that I didn't intend to say, things I hadn't even thought about."

"Like?"

"Like I wanted a divorce." I begin to pace. "That hadn't entered my head. She's mine, I ain't divorcing her. But you know what? She didn't argue. Like she's accepted we're done. Then I told her I was fucking a woman from the club. A woman I've not touched!"

"How did Anna react to that?"

"She was upset. Of course, she was. Christ." I flop down on the posh chair.

"You didn't get around to telling her the truth?" she asks and I shake my head. "You don't need me to tell you that talking to her will make all this go away."

"And then what? She comes home? She sticks by my side?" I snap.

She shrugs her shoulders. "Maybe."

"And I'll spend the rest of my life worrying she came home for the wrong reasons. I've set her free. Released her from the burden."

"A burden isn't how I'd describe it. You think you've set her free, but you haven't given her the option. Anna sounds like a woman who would like the option to make her own choices."

"She's agreed to manage the new bar," I say, changing the subject. She allows me to, which is rare cos usually she pulls me up on that shit. "Well, sort of. She doesn't know the club owns it."

"Is lying the best way to start this off?" she asks.

No. "Yes. She wouldn't take it if she knew the truth."

Eleanor gently places her notepad on the side table and stares at me. "Remember when you said you felt like you'd been tricked by Anna?" I nod. "It upset you enough for the whole thing to snowball out of your control. Isn't this the same sort of thing."

"I know what I'm doing. I know what Anna needs."

She picks the notepad back up, her eyebrows raised slightly. "What would you like to happen next?"

"I want things to go back to how they were before . . ."

"Before Anna? Before Willow? Before the cancer diagnosis?"

I stare down hard at my fingers.

Before all of it.

CHAPTER SIX

ANNA

I don't think it's possible to love a place as much as I do the Easy Riders Bar. Leia was right, this place is amazing. It's small, and we'll get fifty customers at one time tops, but it's intimate, which only adds to the ambiance of the place. Cree hands me a bunch of keys. He spent yesterday showing me around and going through how things work. The most exciting part is I have an office above the bar. That blew me away—I've never had my own office.

"Any problems, call me."

"You?" I repeat. "Not Vinn?" He mutters something vaguely about Vinn being too busy. "Grand opening in a few hours. Exciting," I say. "Are the bar staff going to appear soon?"

"The schedule is pinned behind the bar. One of the guys will be here soon to cover the security side of things. I gotta go. Call if you need anything." I watch Cree rush off and head behind the bar to check out the schedule. I guess that'll be my job from now on. I narrow my eyes when I see Raven's name down for tonight's shift. Just what I need—NOT!

Almost an hour later, Raven turns up looking amazing. She'll get guys in here spending their cash just so they can watch her. I smile stiffly, reminding myself it isn't her fault my husband is an ass and she looks stunning whereas I—I glance down at my jeans and roll my eyes—look so mumsy. "I'm so excited," Raven gushes, looking around.

"I thought you were working in the office for Vinn?" I ask casually.

"Yeah, I am. Office worker by day, bar worker by night. I'm saving hard and I love to be busy."

I show her the office and point to a cupboard where staff can keep their bags and other belongings safe. "Have you done much bar work?" I ask.

"Loads. I really love bar work, chatting to the customers, it's a great job." *Damn, she's just so happy and enthusiastic all the goddamn time!*

The office door opens and Eva marches in. She smiles and throws her arms around me. "This place is fantastic."

I nod. "I'm so excited," I say. Raven slips out the door and goes back down to the bar. "Is she like Superwoman? I mean, she's stunning, she's so nice, she works two jobs. Give me at least one flaw so I can hate on her."

Eva smiles. "Sorry, sweetie, she's really nice. I have nothing to give you. Unless she is shagging your husband, then . . ." She shrugs, leaving the sentence open.

"She's so enthusiastic about working. No wonder Vinn hired her."

"Has Riggs mentioned her since?"

I shake my head. "We haven't spoken about other people. It's not her fault, even if he is going there. I'm not stupid. I know all the women who hang around the club want the President. He's the ultimate prize. Who the hell would turn Riggs down if he came on strong?"

"Me," says Eva bluntly. "I can't even look at him lately. He's an arse."

I grin. "You have to say that because you're my best friend."

The second we open the doors at seven, the place is packed out. Eva steps behind the bar to give us a hand. I make a mental note to double up on staff. I don't have a minute to myself for the first hour but it passes quickly. When I next look up to serve a waiting customer, I stutter, seeing Riggs before me. "Just water," he says in a gravelly voice. "I'm on duty."

I frown, getting him a bottle and placing it on the bar. "Duty?"

"I'm your new doorman baby," he says grinning.

"Since when did you do door work?" I snap. "Did Vinn put you up to this?"

He shakes his head. "My brothers are busy tonight, so I stepped up. Plus, I wanted to be here on opening night. It's a big night for you."

I don't have time for his riddles so I turn to the next customer. Riggs takes his spot at the door. Every time I look up, I see him staring at Raven and my heart breaks a little more. He could at least try and hide how he feels.

An hour before closing, there's a break in customers. Things are slowing down and my aching feet are thankful. "Why don't you take a break, Anna? You haven't moved from this bar all night," says Raven. I smile gratefully, taking her up on the offer. I'd made sure she had regular breaks, I've read up a lot on keeping employees happy.

I step out for some fresh air. "Opening night was a hit," says Riggs. I nod in agreement. The only down side of the evening was watching him watch Raven. "And you're great with the customers."

"I'm surprised you noticed," I mutter.

"Why didn't you do something like this before?" he asks. "You were radiant behind that bar. I've never seen you look so . . . happy."

"I should have," I agree. "I should have made more time for me and what I wanted, instead of you and Reggie. I'm finally getting a life. That makes me happy."

"I'm glad, Anna. I just wish you'd have told me sooner you needed something more. I would have made your dreams come true."

I scoff. "I only wanted you, Riggs. Nothing else mattered. And look where that got me. Are you and Raven happy?" I ask, lightly.

"About that—" he begins, but a scuffle breaks out inside and we both rush to break it up.

Two guys are pushing each other and yelling. There's a woman between them, crying and trying to break them apart. Riggs grabs the nearest guy to him and tries to drag him outside, but he puts up a fight, knocking a table of glasses over. "Come on," I say, groaning at the shards of glass on the floor. "Just calm down."

The guy turns at the same time as Riggs pulls him, and his arm flies up and smashes into my face. A blinding pain rips through my cheek bone and makes my eyeball feel ready to burst. "Motherfucker!" I yell, gripping my cheek. A look of rage passes over Riggs' face and he throws the guy out into the street, following him and closing the door.

Raven puts an arm around my shoulder. "Are you okay?"

I nod as she leads me back behind the bar and grabs a towel. She throws some ice into it and presses it to my cheek. "Shit, he got you good," she mutters, examining my face.

"Can you go out there and make sure Riggs doesn't go mental on the guy? It was an accident." She nods and heads outside to find them. I check my watch to see it's closing time and I'm relieved to ring the bell, letting the customers know to drink up.

It's another ten minutes of waiting for customers to finish their drinks and leave. I follow the final couple to the door so I can lock up. I spot Riggs and Raven chatting in the car park and a stab of jealousy hits me hard. They look good together.

When the pair knock on the door to be let in, I release the latch and go back to collecting dirty glasses. Riggs stands in front of me, blocking my path. He grips my chin in his fingers and tilts my head so he can examine my face, but I pull free and step around him. "I wanna check you're okay," he says as I pile glasses on the bar top.

"I'm all good," I mutter.

"I'll stay and help you clean up. Chains is here to drive Raven home," says Riggs.

"I'm fine by myself," I say, coldly. "You can leave with her."

He stares at me for a second and then begins collecting glasses. Raven appears with her coat and bag. "I enjoyed tonight," she says. "I'll see you tomorrow."

Riggs sees her out to Chains' bike and then returns, locking the door behind him. "You really didn't need to stay," I mutter, loading the glasses into the dishwasher.

"Anna, you'll never be here alone at night."

"You're not responsible for me anymore. I can look after myself."

Riggs wipes down a table. "Mum was really happy you asked her to have the kids tonight. She misses them," he says.

"It'll be weird going home to an empty house," I say. I'll need a lot of childcare help doing this job.

"You're the manager. You can make sure your shifts fit around the kids," he points out.

"I know, but I wanted to be around for the first week or so."

"It suits you," he says quietly. "I couldn't take my eyes off you tonight. I haven't seen you smile like that in a long time."

"I thought you were too busy watching Raven to notice me," I admit.

"I didn't look at her once," he says, frowning. "It's you who I can't take my eyes off, Anna. It's always been you."

"Not always," I almost whisper. "What went wrong with us?" I ask, my tone almost desperate. He rests his hands against the bar. "I thought you'd see Willow and fall in love. That you'd forgive me for all the shit you thought I'd done. But you became so distant, and not just to me but to Willow. She didn't deserve that."

He nods, acknowledging that he agrees, which surprises me. Usually, he shuts me down at this point. "Too much happened and I lost my way," he says. "You took me by surprise when you announced the pregnancy."

"I'm your wife. I didn't need to trap you."

"I know," he mutters. "I said all that stuff because . . ."

"Because what?"

He stares at me for a long while, then sighs. "Come and see the counsellor with me. Please."

I groan. Not this again. "Why?" I ask. "You pushed me away and let me leave, but now, you want to sit in a room with me and a stranger and talk about what? All the things you think I did wrong? You think I'll confess to trapping you? Because I didn't. Willow was an accident, and a good one at that."

"Not about any of that," he snaps. "I wanna work on us. I can't talk to you," he complains.

"I never stopped listening," I snap. "You stopped talking to me and I tried to get you to open up. You went from loving me so fiercely to ignoring me."

"I had shit to deal with," he says bitterly.

"It's all you ever say. You had shit going on, so it meant I had to accept being treated like crap. Well, I've been there before and I refuse to do it again."

He pushes his face in mine. "I am nothing like Reggie. Don't fucking compare me to him. I loved you, but I couldn't tell you everything."

"Loved," I repeat, sucking in a breath, and he steps back. "You said loved, not love." We stare at each other. I place my hand over my throbbing cheek, the pain reminding me of days I spent with Reggie and his violent temper. "We don't need to go to counselling. You've made yourself clear."

RIGGS

I storm out of the bar, punching the wall and then growling in pain. Shit! I need to get a grip. I ain't punched walls since I was a teenager. I shake my hand out and pace.

I couldn't take my eyes off Anna all evening. Seeing her so animated and alive was a beautiful sight. It reminded me of the very first time I saw her, when she marched into my bar demanding I keep my son away from her daughter.

I have two more sessions left at the hospital, two more sessions and my nightmare might be over.

When Anna steps out and locks up, I convince her to get on my bike. It's been so long since she's wrapped her arms around me and held on tight, that I drive the long way to the club, ignoring her when she demands to know why we're going there and not her house. As soon as I park up the bike, she jumps off and pushes her helmet into my chest. "What the hell are you doing?"

A few of the guys are standing outside having a cigarette, pretending not to listen in. "I thought you'd want to be here for the kids tomorrow?"

"Bullshit," she snaps. "Your mum is dropping them for me tomorrow, you knew that."

"I have an appointment with Eleanor first thing. You're coming too."

"Who?" she growls.

"My counsellor."

She grips her fists into balls and her face reddens with rage. "You can't force me to go there. How dare you just decide what I'm doing."

"I can and I am," I say confidently. She begins to march towards the gates and I smile to myself. I love it when she's angry like this. I feel my cock stir. It takes me by surprise cos since my treatment started, I've been lucky to even get half a semi. I race after her, snatching her arm and spinning her to me, then I bend and throw her over my shoulder like a rag doll and march with her into the club.

I head straight for our room. It's exactly how she left it because I haven't slept in here since she walked out. I throw her on the unmade bed and she bounces a couple of times before pushing herself up to sit. "You can't make all this right. We're over," she mutters.

"We'll see," I say, shrugging out of my kutte.

"I've told you a million times, I can't put myself through it anymore. Your moods and temper. I can't live on the edge like that wondering if you'll wake up loving me or hating me."

I stop undressing and stare down at her. "I've been fucking up for months. I know I have. Shit's got on top of me with the club and Leia." I shake my head. "I've not been myself."

"Stop talking," she mutters. "But I want to make it right. I want us to try and sort this mess out. I want to be there for you and the kids.""I said, stop talking."

"Anna—"

She pushes up from the bed. "I said, stop fucking talking," she hisses. She prods a finger to my chest. "Months, I've cried over you. I've begged you to talk to me. I've degraded myself to try and get you to fuckin' notice me and you haven't. I've left three times. Three!" Her face is red with anger as she continues to prod my chest. "And I am done! I don't want to hear how you're sorry. How you had shit to deal with, because guess what, so did I. You were so busy avoiding me that you forgot I was carrying your child. You stood there," she says, pointing to a spot on the bedroom floor, "and watched me pack up my clothes, crying and telling you I was done. You didn't stop me. Yah know why?" she asks, and I shake my head, scared to interrupt her rant. "Because you stopped loving me." I try to protest, but she holds up her hand and I think better of it. "And I'm okay with that."

Now would be the right time to explain myself. I open my mouth to say the words but they don't come. I try a second time and she stares expectantly but I close my mouth. I don't want her to come back out of pity. Once the treatment is finished, I don't have to tell her a thing. "I'm sorry you think that," I eventually say, "but we're going to the counsellor tomorrow. Now, get some sleep."

Her eyes widen and I turn away, continuing to undress. "Did you sleep with someone else?" she asks. "I've been wanting to ask since the first time you rejected me. I was wearing a new red lace bodice. You looked me up and down and told me you weren't feeling well. I watched you get into bed and turn your back to me. I asked you what was wrong and you said I wouldn't understand."

"I remember," I mutter. She looked sexy and it killed me to turn her away, but it was my first day of treatment and I was so tired and weak.

"And I cried silent tears beside you, wondering if you'd had sex with another woman and guilt was eating you alive. Is that it? Did you cheat?"

"I haven't had sex with another woman," I say firmly. "I haven't cheated on you."

"Except with Raven," she says.

"Not even with Raven," I confirm.

"Just because we separated, doesn't mean it's okay to have sex with another woman. We're still married."

"I haven't had sex with her," I say. "I swear on Ziggy's life."

"I don't even know why we're discussing this. It doesn't matter anymore."

"Have you had sex with another man?" I ask and brace myself for her answer.

"Would you give a shit if I had?" she asks.

My fists clench and hot rage burns through my body. "I'd kill any man who laid a finger on you. You're mine," I hiss.

She rolls her eyes. "To think that used to make me feel safe and loved. Now, it boils my blood."

"We're getting nowhere like this." I sigh. "Let's sleep. We can talk tomorrow."

She shakes her head. "No."

"No?" I repeat.

She pushes past me and heads for the door. "I need a drink."

CHAPTER SEVEN

ANNA

"Someone looks tired," says Eva.

"Why are you still awake?" I ask, looking around the club bar. It's almost one in the morning and the club is quiet with only a few brothers hanging around.

"Sometimes I just need space, yah know?" she mutters.

I frown. "Things okay with you and Cree?" I ask.

She nods and forces a smile. "Things are good," she says and I raise a brow in doubt. She's quick to put me right. "No, they really are. I've just never had a guy be so full-on. He's . . ." she pauses, looking for the right word. "Obsessed."

"With you or sex?"

"Both," she says, smiling. "I'm not saying it's a bad thing cos I love him, I really love him, but sometimes he's too much and I have to take a break. He's always nearby, always within my eyeline. In bed, he wraps himself around me, it's like he's scared I'm gonna disappear."

"Have you talked to him about it?" I ask.

She shakes her head. "He doesn't like to talk, you know what he's like. I'm thinking of speaking to his counsellor," she says.

I roll my eyes. "Maybe I can help there. Riggs is forcing me into seeing her with him."

"He can't force you to talk," she says, shrugging.

"A part of me wants to go just so I can say it in front of her. Maybe then she can explain it to him because he sure as shit isn't understanding it from me," I mutter.

"Say what?"

"That I'm done. That I'm happy, and for once in my life, it doesn't involve a man."

"Wow," says Eva. "That's huge. Good for you. You don't love him?"

"I'll always love him. But I'm done trying to be his wife. He's hurt me too much. At least with Reggie, I knew what he was like. His physical abuse was what I expected. Riggs, he drew me in and then turned. He's hurt me more than Reggie's fists ever could."

Eva sucks in a breath and her eyes widen. I wince and slowly turn to see who she's looking at, even though I've already guessed that Riggs is there. He stares at me for a long minute, a range of emotions pass over his face. "I'll take you home," he mutters. My heart twinges again and Eva gives me a sympathetic smile.

Outside, he hands me a helmet and gets on the bike without looking at me. I stand beside him. "Riggs," I begin.

"Forget it, Anna. Get on."

"I didn't mean—"

"I know what you meant. Get on." He's staring straight ahead rigidly and his hands are gripping the handlebars tight. I decide it isn't worth pushing and I get on the bike. He shifts uncomfortably, stiffening when I wrap my arms around him. It breaks my heart all over again, reminding me of how things got between us before I left.

He stops outside my house but makes no move to get off the bike. I hand him my helmet and smile sadly. "If I knew you were there, I wouldn't have been so harsh," I say.

"Then maybe it's a good thing I was. Sorry I was so pushy. I'll go and see my solicitor after my session with Eleanor tomorrow. I'll get the papers drawn up." He drives off before I can answer him.

The sun rises and I haven't had a wink of sleep. I send a text off to Frankie, asking her to hold onto the girls a while longer. I hit the gym hard, something I haven't done for a long time. I head home after and change into jeans and a soft pink knitted jumper. I want to look presentable, although I'm not sure why it matters.

I finally arrive and wait outside patiently. At exactly ten, Riggs stops his bike outside Eleanor's office. His eyes narrow on me as he pulls his helmet off. "What the fuck are you doing here?"

I knew he'd react badly, because he lashes out with words when he's hurt. "Are we going inside or what?" I ask.

"You made yourself perfectly clear last night, Anna. I'm seeing my solicitor straight after this appointment."

"Then maybe we can go together." I smile and head up the steps, pressing the buzzer to Eleanor's office.

Eleanor smiles warmly. Riggs stares out of the large office window as I take a seat. "It's so good to finally meet you, Anna. Riggs wasn't sure you'd come."

"I almost didn't," I admit. "I sat up the whole night thinking of reasons not to come."

"But you came. What was the reason for that?" she asks.

I glance over at Riggs, who's watching me from the corner of his eye. "I guess if there's still love, there's still hope, right?"

Eleanor smiles, nodding. "I agree. How do you feel, Finn?"

"Numb," he mutters. "Pissed."

"You wanted Anna to come," says Eleanor.

"I overheard her comparing me to her abusive ex last night. She's here right now out of guilt."

"That's not true," I mutter. "I didn't mean to compare you. I was just telling Eva that you've hurt me so much more by pushing me away than Reggie ever did by hitting me. It wasn't how I wanted it to sound."

"You're allowed to feel that way," says Eleanor. "We all feel pain differently. You're feeling that mentally your pain is worse than physical pain." I nod in agreement. "That's because you feel the aftermath of a physical pain, say a bruise, is easier to heal than your heart." I nod again. She's good. "Forget all the bullshit," snaps Riggs and we both turn to him. "Are we done or not?"

I hesitate and he sneers. Eleanor takes a breath and releases it slowly. "Anna is here, that counts for something. It sounds like you've both said some hurtful things in the past. If we keep going over them, you'll never move forward. Anna, would you be willing to see me separately sometime?" she asks.

"I don't . . . urm . . . think that—"

"She doesn't think it's her thing," snaps Riggs. "I'd like to see you just once, and if you still feel the same, then don't come back," says Eleanor, smiling. "Free of charge for the first session."

I find myself nodding. "Tell you what, have this session," says Riggs, heading for the door. "It's clear we don't need it."

I stand to go after him, but Eleanor shakes her head. "He walks out a lot," she says. "I challenge his thinking and he sometimes takes a breather. He'll be back."

"He's so hot headed," I mutter.

"I imagine that can take its toll on your relationship."

"Lately, I don't know which Riggs will surface. Some days he's amazing, and others, he can barely look at me. He used to be so in love with me, he'd suffocate me with affection."

"Can you think back to a time in your relationship when that stopped?"

I nod. "The day I announced I was pregnant with Willow."

"Did Riggs want a child?"

I shake my head. "We agreed to wait, but I was sick and missed the pill. It wasn't intentional, but when I did the test, I thought he'd be pleased. Or at least, if he wasn't, he'd come around to the idea."

"And he didn't?" she asks.

"No. He accused me of trying to trap him. Said I'd gotten pregnant on purpose. I'm sure he told you about Michelle and how she left him and Ziggy." Eleanor nods. "So I understand why he panicked. He's been through a lot."

"It sounds like you have too," she says. "Your ex doesn't sound like a nice man."

I haven't thought about Reggie properly in such a long time. Since I left Riggs, I've started getting letters from him. I haven't opened any, but I know his handwriting. I knew he'd resurface once I touched his money. The fact he has my address doesn't even surprise me anymore. "He can't hurt me anymore. He'll never get out of prison again."

"Sometimes, when men treat us badly, it can scar us in other ways."

I shrug. "I've been mistreated by men most of my life, so I'm used to it."

"When Finn let you down by accusing you of trapping him, that wasn't a surprise to you?" she asks. "It was," I say. "But I guess him letting me down wasn't. I thought he'd be happy when I told him. When it became clear he wasn't going to come around, I realised he was just another arse to let me down. But I got over it. I'm a good mum, and Willow and Malia will be fine. I used to think I needed a man in my life, but I'm seeing now that I don't."

"Do you have contact with Reggie?"

I shake my head. "He writes, but I don't open his letters."

"Does Finn know about the letters?" she asks and I shake my head again. "How would he react to that news?"

"Right now?" I ask and she nods. "He wouldn't care."

"Why do you think he asked you to come to this session?"

I shrug. "Maybe so he can say he tried. The old ladies at the club give him hassle about our break-up. They blame him. It was both of us, but they blame him."

"Both of you?" she asks. "I should have taken precautions after the unprotected sex, after I was sick. I thought it would be fine, but it wasn't. When he told me he wasn't happy about the pregnancy, I should have taken care of it."

"An abortion?"

"Maybe. It's all such a mess. He's not himself and he doesn't talk to me. I don't know how to help him. Frankie, his mum, tells me it's just how the men in the club get. Club life can be brutal for them and I should just be there for him. I try, I really do. Maybe I'm not cut out for club life. I'm not good enough or strong enough to be someone's old lady, especially not the president."

"You're stronger than you realise," says Eleanor. "You chose to leave two men and put you and your children first. That takes strength. Don't be too hard on yourself."

RIGGS

I sit on the wall, waiting patiently for Anna. She's been in there over an hour and I wonder what the fuck they found to talk about. When she finally surfaces, I see she's been crying. I jump off the wall and head for my bike. When she doesn't follow, I narrow my eyes. "Thought you wanted to come to the solicitor's?"

"Let's leave that for now," she mutters. "I think we should go, at least get the ball rolling," I say. She eventually nods and gets on the bike.

The solicitor is blunt. He gives us some advice but tells us we need separate solicitors, that he can't advise us both because it's a conflict of interests. We leave feeling deflated and we're both quiet. I check my watch. "I have an appointment. I don't have time to take you home. I'll get you a cab," I say. "No, it's fine. I'm going to see my friend and then I'm meeting your mum with the kids."

I nod and kiss her on the forehead. It's a natural thing to do and it feels bittersweet. "Thanks for coming today. Are you seeing her again?"

Anna shrugs. "I don't know." She begins to walk away and then turns back to face me. "Reggie has written to me. I know you hate secrets and I feel like it's something I should tell you."

"How long has he been writing? What does he want?" "Six letters over the last few weeks. I haven't opened them."

I nod stiffly. "I'll collect the letters later." I watch her walk away. That fucker's got a nerve after what he did to Anna. My blood boils knowing he's got her new address. That means he has contacts watching her.

By the time I get to the hospital, I'm raging. Before, if I felt like this, I'd fuck. It was the only way to bring me down and stop my path of self-destruction. Now, I can't even do that.

The radiation therapist shakes my hand. We're becoming friends, if that's possible, as these sessions have been taking place almost every day for the last few months. We do the usual shit, an MRI and then treatment. Then I head to the restroom. Sometimes I leave straight away, but today, I want to see if Cal's around. I met him at the start of my journey. He was already three weeks into treatment and we got to chatting on one of my first visits. He hadn't told anyone in his family either, so we kind of formed a friendship based on supporting each other and keeping a huge secret.

He isn't in the restroom, but I take a seat anyway to wait for him. He sometimes arrives a little later than me. I have my head resting back and my eyes closed when I hear the sound of her laughter. My heart skips a beat. Fuck, I'm even hearing her in my daydreams. I laugh to myself, but when I open my eyes, there's Anna, staring at me with wide eyes. A second later, Cal comes in, grinning when he spots me.

"Brother, how was it today? I had that hot nurse, but it was brutal," he says, patting my shoulder and seating himself next to me. "At one point, I . . ." he trails off when he sees me and Anna staring at each other. A female standing with Anna gently takes her by the arm, startling her. She shakes her head, like she's clearing a bad dream, and follows the woman without another word.

"Who was that hot piece of ass?" asks Cal. "My wife," I mutter, watching the two women leave the room.

※※※ ※※※

I don't bother going to Anna's to collect Reggie's letters. I can't face the questions and I'm exhausted. Proton therapy causes me some serious fatigue. Raven spots me making my way through the club and follows me until we get upstairs. "How was it?" she asks.

"Anna was there," I mutter, and her eyes bug out of her head.

I open my bedroom door and she follows me in. "Shit. Did you tell her?"

I shake my head. "She walked away before I could. She was there with someone, a woman. I think we were both too shocked."

"You have to tell her, Riggs." "I have one more fucking session. Why the fuck was she there?" I growl, slamming my hand against the wall.

Raven sighs, grabbing my hand and examining the cuts left from where I punched the wall. "Get some rest. You look terrible. We'll come up with a plan. And stop punching shit, it won't help."

I shake my head. "I ain't telling her. If she asks, I'll refuse to tell her."

"That's a dumb idea," mutters Raven. "You tried that with me, remember? Anna knows you better than me, so she'll work it out, if she hasn't already. And maybe," she pauses, "maybe this happened for a reason. It's a shove in the right direction. Now is your chance to open up and tell her everything."

I lie down. In the beginning, I didn't tell Anna because we were dealing with the pregnancy thing. Then it became too hard to talk. Eventually, I decided to keep it to myself. Call me pig-headed, but since treatment for my prostate cancer began, I've felt less and less like a man. I can't even have a fucking wank. I groan out loud and Raven smiles at me sympathetically.

"Maybe this will make things better between you."

"Exactly," I snap. "She'll feel sorry for me and come back. I don't want that. Anna's too kind and caring to walk away. She'll stay out of pity."

Raven rolls her eyes. "Sleep, Pres. Worry about the rest later."

CHAPTER EIGHT

ANNA

I've tried calling his phone a million times, but he won't answer. I'd gone to the hospital to see one of my former foster mums. I'd found out she'd gotten cancer and promised to pop in and see her. I wasn't expecting to see Riggs there, and I left in shock. But it's been three days and I've not seen him to ask what the hell is going on. That's why I've asked Eva to come over and watch the girls for me. I'm on a mission and I'm going to find out everything, once and for all.

I get to the club and Cree is outside smoking a cigarette. "Anna," he says, sounding surprised. "I thought you were seeing Eva at your place tonight?"

"Don't worry, Cree. She's exactly where she said she'd be. She's watching the kids for me. I've come to see Riggs."

He winces. "Probably not a good idea. He's been drinking today."

"I can handle him," I say, heading inside.

Riggs is sitting on the couch with a club girl resting on his lap, placing kisses along his jaw. I watch them for a minute, feeling everyone's eyes on me. I won't give them a show—I'm not that sort of girl. Instead, I stand in front of them. The girl panics, jumping up from his lap and rushing off. It isn't her fault, he's the President, and she can't say no to him if she wants to carry on staying at the club. I place my hands on my hips and Riggs stares up at me with a stupid smirk on his face. "Here she is," he grins. "Come to ruin the party, my love?"

I call over to Lake and Chains. "Get him up," I order. They exchange a wary look.

"Do as she says," comes Frankie's voice, and I suppress the urge to smile as they move to Riggs, taking an arm each and lifting him from the couch.

"Upstairs," I say.

I lead the way to our bedroom. It's a mess. I push the bathroom door open and turn on the shower. "In there," I say, and they push him under the spray of water fully clothed. He splutters, trying to suck in some air but getting a mouthful of water instead. "I need coffee and water," I say and Lake rushes off. After a few minutes, Chains helps Riggs from the shower and guides him to a chair by the window. "I'll take it from here," I say and he gives me a relieved smile. "Ask Lake to leave the coffee outside the door."

I wait for Chains to leave, then I slowly unfasten the buttons on Riggs' shirt. He's half asleep and doesn't stir as I undress him. I go to tug his wet jeans down his legs, and that's when I see the large red mark on his abdomen. I'm at eye level, so there's no avoiding it. I gently run a finger over the area, as he flinches slightly but doesn't fuss. I finish getting him out of the wet clothes and pull on a fresh pair of boxer shorts. "This is what I mean," he slurs. "You'll become a fucking nurse to me." I help him over to the bed and he half sits up against the headboard.

"Tell me everything," I say, fetching the coffee and water from outside the room. He takes the coffee with shaky hands. "From the beginning," I add.

"I'm one of the statistics," he mutters. "You know, only four in ten men get prostate cancer in their thirties? Most men get it in their sixties, but no, not me."

I suck in a breath and climb onto the bed, facing him. I tuck my legs underneath myself and resist the urge to throw my arms around him. "I was pissing all the goddamn time. I'd piss and need another in ten minutes. It drove me nuts, and I remember Raven asking me about it. She was in The Windsor with us and I went to the toilet three times in twenty minutes. She said she knew a guy who was like that and he'd been diagnosed with cancer. I laughed. As if that could happen to me. I have a wife and kids to look after, a club to run, it wasn't gonna be me. But she nagged me, said I needed to get checked out or she'd tell you and Mum." He pauses, drinking the rest of his coffee and setting the cup down on the bedside table.

"Why didn't you tell me?" I whisper.

"Cos you announced you were fucking pregnant the very same day I got my test results. My head was fucked. I'd been with a doctor telling me I might have to have a fucking colostomy bag for life, that I'd probably never get a fucking erection on my own again let alone have any more kids, and then you stood beside me, smiling and laughing, and told the club we were having a kid. And I just went into shock."

Tears silently fall down my cheeks. "I didn't know," I mumble.

"Part of me didn't wanna take your smile away, you were so happy. Then I ended up doing exactly that by pushing you away. When I left, before you had Willow, I told the club I was hitting the road for a while.

I was actually having an operation to see if they could remove any of the cancer. They got most of it, but they've been giving me proton therapy to target that area. The last one was two days ago. Now, I've gotta wait to see if they've gotten it all or if I have to try something else."

"Like chemotherapy?" I ask, my voice shaky. I'd been searching up cancer treatments since I saw him at the hospital.

He nods. "And if I have that, the chance of us ever having another kid is unlikely."

"I don't care about having more kids," I say. "You're the most important thing in all this."

He shakes his head with a look of disgust on his face. "I don't expect you to stick around, Anna. I'm not the man you married."

I shuffle closer and place a hand against his cheek. "Don't say that. Why didn't you tell me? All this could have been avoided."

"I don't want you with me out of pity. I can't get a fucking erection. You know how that makes me feel?"

"None of that matters. I love you. I don't care about the sex or kids."

He pushes my hand away from his face. "You will. In time. I don't know if things will get better or a shit tonne worse. I don't want you looking after me. I never wanted you to know. Now that you do, I don't feel better for it. Now, I'm stressed about you and how you'll cope. Just walk away. It's less complicated when you aren't around."

I recoil like he's slapped me. "That's not fair. You never gave me a chance to stay and fight for us with the whole truth out. If you'd have told me, I could have understood your behaviour. I thought you hated me, that you'd stopped loving me!"

"Maybe I have. Maybe that's why I couldn't bring myself to tell you."

I swipe my tears away. "Stop pushing me away," I snap. "It's cruel."

"I mean, how messed up is it that Raven noticed and you didn't? What does that say about us?" A physical pain swells in my chest. I know he's being like this so I'll walk away, and right now, I'm considering it. "She's been around, yah know, asking how I am. Making sure I rest and everyone leaves me the hell alone." I can't stop the flow of tears anymore. "She did the job you should have done."

"Stop," I whisper. "No more."

"And she's pretty, right? If my erection is gonna come back, then surely it'll work for her."

I clench my fists because slapping his smartass face will only make me feel shittier. His cruel eyes glare at me. He expects me to run. Instead, I lie beside him and leave my tears to fall. He should witness what his cruel words do to me.

RIGGS

I stare straight ahead, fixing my angry glare at the window. Why won't she fucking leave? Her quiet sobs shake the bed. I'm angry she's found out the truth. Now, she'll hang around and I won't know if that's because she wants to be here out of love or if she feels duty-bound cos we're married. I haven't stopped drinking since my last round of therapy. I shouldn't even be fucking drinking, but who was gonna stop me?

"Is it something I do?" she eventually whispers. When I don't answer, she continues, "Am I the problem?"

"What do you mean?" I ask, sighing impatiently.

"Is it something I do to make men treat me like shit?"

Her words cut me like a knife to the heart. "No," I mutter.

"Then why does it happen to me? When will I meet a guy who treats me like . . ." She pauses, thinking. "Like Vinn treats Leia?"

I scoff. "Vinn isn't even with Leia. He's just obsessed."

"But he treats her so well. He doesn't care that she's with Chains. He would do anything for her. He even put me in one of his houses just because she asked him to."

"Anna, you don't do anything wrong," I mutter. I feel like a shit bag. I drink the glass of water as my head feels fuzzy. "You just fall for arses like me."

"You treated me like that once," she says. "When we first met, I thought the world of you. You stuck me on a pedestal. Maybe that's why it feels so much worse—you put me up so high and then kicked it from under me. Now, I don't know how to get back to the woman you fell in love with."

"You shouldn't want to," I say. "You deserve better."

"It breaks my heart to know you didn't trust me enough to tell me about this. I didn't notice like Raven did. I guess I was too busy trying to be the perfect Pres's wife. I wanted to make sure I was doing everything right, like your mum did for your dad. She gives so many tips, sometimes, I feel like I'm in way over my head." She smiles, but it's sad and empty. "Don't ask too many questions, Anna. Make sure you're there to listen, Anna. Don't make decisions about Ziggy, Anna, but don't pester the Pres with unimportant shit. You just have to stroke his ego, Anna, make him feel special so he doesn't turn to a club girl." She winces as fresh tears fall. "I got it all so wrong. I stopped being myself. I wanted to be like the other ol' ladies, but it didn't even work because in the end, you couldn't talk to me."

Guilt eats away at me and I pull her against my chest. She sobs harder. "I didn't know you were under so much pressure," I say into her hair. "I fell in love with you because you weren't like the other women here. I liked that."

"The women have so many rules. Rules for how to behave around other charters. How to fuck, depending on the mood of your man.

Shit, they even decide what food to cook depending on what mood you're in. This whole club works around you and how to please you. I feel so insignificant because I don't know what rules apply when. We stopped having fun. We stopped laughing together."

I nod. "We're both guilty of that," I say.

"Would you ever have told me, if I hadn't seen you at the hospital?"

I shake my head. "No."

"And you haven't told anyone, not even Cree?"

I shake my head again. "Just Raven."

Anna pushes herself to sit. "I'm glad you finally told me, even though you didn't want to. I'm only sorry you felt you couldn't sooner. If you need anything, anything at all, I'm here." She stands and I have a second to make a decision. I can't let her leave. Not again.

CHAPTER NINE

ANNA

I feel so exhausted from our talk. My eyes are swollen and sore from crying and my heart is in tatters . . . again. All this time, he's been suffering and he couldn't even tell me. I feel like a failure and a shitty wife. As I turn to leave, I feel his fingers wrapping around my wrist. "You're not leaving," he says, his voice firm. He pulls me back onto the bed. "You're talking like it's final. Like you can just walk out of here and pretend nothing's changed." He wraps himself around me, my back to his chest, and presses his nose into my hair. We lay in silence for a few minutes. "It was easier to talk to Raven," he whispers, and I try to pull away, but he holds me tighter against his body. "Relax," he hisses. "It was easier because there's no connection with her. She doesn't look at me with puppy dog eyes like I'm crushing her whole world. Fuck, Anna, there's no one that's gonna replace you. You're my world."

"Everything's such a mess," I mumble.

"You said, if there's still love, then there's still hope."

"What do I know," I say briskly.

"You know I love you. That never stopped. And you love me."

"Do you, Riggs?" I ask. "I haven't felt like you've loved me in a long time."

"Apparently, I project," he says and I frown. "Least that's what Eleanor tells me. I projected my anger and hurt from Michelle onto you. My situation with her and Ziggy made me fear the same would happen with you and Willow. My behaviour was pushing you away, so if it happened again, it wouldn't hurt me as much. I did it subconsciously, not intentionally."

"The end result was still the same. I love my kids. I love yours. I've treated Ziggy like my own. I'd never leave my kids."

"I know," he mutters. "With everything else happening, I lost sight of shit. I stressed myself out thinking you'd leave the kids and I'd drop dead and then they'd lose us both." He shifts and I feel his cock pushing into my back. "Don't get any ideas," he mutters. "It won't stay."

"How do we stop it happening again?" I ask. "We can't keep putting the kids through this. Malia and Ziggy will end up messed up."

"I can't concentrate," he mumbles into my hair as he pushes his erection against my ass. "It's been too long since this has happened." I smile. It should be the last thing on either of our minds, but I wiggle my ass against him anyway. "That ain't helping," he mutters.

"Maybe we should see what happens. If it turns out to be a false alarm, then so what," I say, shrugging.

"I'd feel like less of a man," he admits. "If I can't please my wife."

I move his hand to cup my breast. "I don't think you'll have a problem with that," I whisper. "I seem to recall you were good with your tongue."

I feel his body shake as a laugh escapes him. "There is that."

His hand moves around behind my ass and he pushes up my dress, then gently tugs my panties down my legs. He pulls my ass closer to him and lines himself up at my entrance. "It might not work," he mutters.

"Then I have a perfectly good vibrator we can play with instead," I say, trying to ease the pressure he's putting on himself. He enters me in one swift move, causing my breath to leave my body. I grip the pillow and push my face into it to stifle the moan of pleasure that escapes me.

"Shit, you have no idea how good that feels," he pants, digging his fingers into my hip. He rolls on top of me, so I'm on my stomach, and begins to move, grabbing my ass hard as he thrusts inside me. "I never appreciated your pussy so much," he groans.

It takes just minutes for me to reach my orgasm. It's been so long since he touched me, just hearing his pleasure sends me spiralling over the edge. He follows, pulling from me right before he comes, spilling his pleasure onto my back. His heavy pants fill the room as he rubs the evidence of his arousal into my skin. "Mine," he whispers.

"Yours," I mutter.

RIGGS

I feel lighter, either because I've finally told Anna everything or because I've managed to fuck her. I don't care about the reason, all I know is it feels good. We lie together, her head against my chest. "What happens now?" she asks. If there's one thing I've learned from Eleanor, it's not to rush things.

"I want us to see Eleanor together. We both have issues we gotta face." I feel her nod. "No more running," I add. "We have to try harder to make us work."

"What if you get bad news from your final test results?"

I run my fingers along her back. "We'll cross that bridge when we come to it. One day at a time."

"What about Reggie?" I ask.

"What about him? Burn the letters. There's nothing he's gotta say that we need to hear. But we have to be cautious, cos he's clearly got someone watching you or feeding back information. You need a brother on you all the time. You and Malia."

"I think I should stay living where I am for now," she says quietly.

"For now," I agree. "But not forever. We're gonna work this out. I need you in my life."

She snuggles tighter against me. "I have to get back. Eva is watching the girls."

I sigh. Everything in me wants to order her to move back here so I have access to her twenty-four-seven, but if we rush this, we'll end up back here in a few months. We have to face our demons.

"I can't drive, I've had too much to drink. I'll get a prospect to take you."

"Riggs, can we keep this between us?" she asks. I bristle at her words, but she gently strokes my arm. "I'm not ashamed. I just feel like when everyone gets involved, it becomes complicated. Let's see how things go for a while before we make any big announcements."

I nod. Big announcements are what started all this.

CHAPTER TEN

ANNA

Eva grins the second I walk through the door. "Well, look at the glow on you," she says.

I subconsciously rub my cheeks and blush. "We talked."

"Please," she scoffs. "You did much more than talk. How did he worm his way out of it?"

I shrug. "We talked. We cleared the air. We needed that. I've agreed to see the counsellor with him again."

"That sounds like a plan."

"He kept something from me, something huge," I say and she eyes me suspiciously. "I can't tell you, it isn't my thing to tell. But he told someone else, confided in her, and it bothers me. Do I say something to her or leave it?"

Eva purses her lips, thinking for a minute. "Is she a threat to your relationship?"

I shrug again. "Honestly, I don't know. In one way, I should thank her for spotting something I didn't, but in another, I'm mad she didn't tell me."

"Then say that. Speak from the heart and be honest. If you don't get it off your chest, you'll be eaten up with it."

I don't sleep well. My mind is replaying everything Riggs told me. What if the treatment hasn't worked? We've spent so long being apart and playing stupid games that we might have lost our chance.

I toss and turn the entire night again, and when the sun rises, Willow wakes and I'm lost in baby stuff. When the rest of the population rises at a more reasonable hour, I send a text off to Raven asking her to meet me in the park.

I like Raven. It's hard not to like her. I know Leia has her issues, with Raven and Chains being close friends, but even she struggles to pick fault with the redheaded beauty. I smile as she walks towards me. "Hey," she says, taking a seat and peering into Willow's pushchair. "She's getting so big," she points out.

"I know about Riggs," I say, and she eyes me. "He told me everything last night."

"That's good," she says warily. "What did he tell you exactly?"

"About the cancer," I say, and she looks relieved. "I want to thank you," I begin as she frowns. "You noticed enough to ask him to go and get checked. If you hadn't," I shrug, "well, maybe he still wouldn't know."

"I'm glad he got checked and he's having treatment."

"I also wanted to say something else." I bite my lower lip, choosing my words carefully. "You must be watching him pretty closely to notice how often he goes to the bathroom," I say, and she hangs her head, her cheeks turning crimson. "I get it," I continue. "He's the President, he's charming, good looking. It's hard not to fancy him."

"I've never once made a move," she blurts out quickly. "I wouldn't."

I nod. "Good. I just wanted you to know that I see it. I love him, despite what it might look like from the outside. We're married and we have Willow. I'm asking you, woman to woman, stay away from my husband."

"I have, I promise. I respect you, Anna. I'd never go there, I swear. He doesn't know how I feel, and I've not made a single move on him."

"Let's keep it that way."

Riggs is in my office already when I arrive at Easy Riders later that day. He closes his laptop and looks at me. "I have a confession," he says.

I place my bag by the side of the desk. "Okay."

"I own this place. Well, the club does."

My mouth falls open. "I thought Vinn owned it?"

"I had to tell Leia that because I knew you wouldn't come and work here otherwise. I needed a manager and you were doing the course, it was an obvious choice, and if you'd have told me months ago how you felt about getting a job, I would have done it sooner."

"I wanted to get my independence," I argue.

"And you have that. You earn your money here, Anna. The figures look great," he says. "And if you fuck up, I'll fire you. No special treatment," he adds, grinning.

"Talking of doing a great job," I say, taking a seat opposite him. "I'm thinking of making some changes to the staff."

"I'm listening."

"Raven, for example," I say, casually. "Nothing against her, but I'd like some new faces around."

Riggs frowns. "The customers love Raven. She's great behind the bar."

"I'm just not comfortable around her at the moment," I admit.

"Then change your shifts so you aren't together, Anna. You can't let personal shit get in the way."

"I thought you said I was the manager, therefore, I should make the decisions, right?"

I watch him gather his things. He kisses me on the cheek. "Baby, you are, but it's a stupid idea. Raven is good for this place." He leaves the office. The truth is, I want to limit her time around Riggs as much as possible.

RIGGS

I find Raven in the cellar changing a barrel. "Things okay with you and Anna?" I ask, and she jumps at the sound of my voice.

"Yep," she says, smiling awkwardly.

I step closer and she takes a step back. "You're lying."

"She warned me off you today, okay. She was marking her territory."

I smile. I like that she's marking me as hers. It means we're making progress. "We're sorting our shit out. She knows there's nothing between us but let her do her thing. Anna likes you, she'll settle down." I make my way back to the office and find Anna chatting away on her laptop. I move closer, her eyes fixed on the video call. "I like the first set of flyers better," she says. "Hold those up again."

I place my hand on her knee and she smirks. "And the third set," she says. I crouch down, nudging her skirt higher and higher until my hands reach her silk panties. She tries to discreetly bat my hands away. "No, it's the first set. Let's talk numbers," she says. I place a kiss on her inner thigh and she parts her legs, allowing me more room. I grin, running my fingers over her panties. She gasps but covers it with a cough. The man on the video call is talking about prices as I slip a finger underneath the silk and find her wet. I suck my finger into my mouth and hum in approval—she tastes amazing.

"I have to go. Can you email me those numbers?" she squeaks. I don't wait for him to answer before I'm tugging down her panties. She cancels the call just as I bury my head between her legs. "Christ, Riggs, I thought you said it wasn't working," she mutters, burying her hands in my hair.

"It wasn't. You do things to me," I say, opening my jeans and pushing them down my hips. I pull her down to the floor and she wraps her legs around me. "They said I might never get it working again, yet here we are. I've had some hormone shit pumped into me. The doc'll be pleased when I tell him it's working," I smirk as she sinks down onto me. She feels fucking amazing. "I knew the office was a good idea," I add and she laughs.

CHAPTER ELEVEN

RIGGS

I've never felt more thankful for having Anna than I do right now. I'm gripping her hand so tight, her fingers are white, but I can't seem to let her go. The doctor breezes into his office and shakes hands with us both. "How are you feeling?" he asks.

"Good. Best I've been in months," I say.

"Any concerns?"

I shake my head. "Everything seems to be working," I say, nodding down to my cock. The doc smirks and Anna gasps.

"Well, that's good news. I told you, younger patients tend to recover much quicker than older ones. I have to say, Finn, I'm impressed with how well you've fought this." He pulls some papers from a file. "The tests show your levels are healthy, which indicates you're in the clear."

I suck in a breath and Anna smiles wide. "That doesn't mean we're signing you off," he adds quickly. "Your treatment is over, and provided your PSA levels remain low, we'll be happy just to monitor you every few months. I've spoken to colleagues and we feel that at the moment, you won't require another dose of hormone injections to reduce your testosterone levels. But, any signs, and you know what they are, you have to come straight back. No waiting."

I nod, hardly believing the relief I feel. "I don't know what to say," I mutter.

"Congratulations, Finn. And well done." He leans over the desk and shakes my hand again.

We step outside and Anna throws her arms around me. "I can't believe it!"

"Me either," I say. "I was convinced it'd be bad news. I gotta go back and tell Cree."

"Cree knows?" she asks.

I shake my head. "I promised myself I'd tell him once I was clear. I need to explain why I haven't been myself," I explain, and she smiles, gently squeezing my arm.

"I love you," she says.

I kiss her, gripping her perfect face in my hands. "I love you so much," I whisper against her lips. "And I'm so sorry for everything I've put you through. I can't take back what I did but I can try and make up for it. If you'll let me.""From now on, we talk. Your problems are my problems and vice versa. You pushed me away to try and save me from hurting and yet you made it ten times worse. I'm your wife. We face these things together."

I nod. Kissing her again. I've been an arse, there's no doubting that. I pushed my wife away when I should have been confiding in her, letting her support me. I've missed out on months with my baby girl because I was too scared of dying and leaving her. I felt less of a man because cancer made me vulnerable and I hated that feeling.

Getting the results today feels like I've been given a second chance at life, and now I have to put right all of my wrongs. I need to get my head back in the game and run my club like the leader I once was. With Anna back by my side, I know it's possible. We're not perfect, and we have a long way to go to get back to where we were, but I'm thankful she's giving me another try. I can't let her down again. She's my queen, now, forever, always . . . because where there's love, there's hope.

THE END

A note from me to you

If you enjoyed Riggs' Saviour, please share the love. Tell everyone by leaving a review or rating on Amazon, Goodreads, or wherever else you find it. You can also follow me on social media. I'm literally everywhere, but here's my linktr.ee to make it easier.

https://linktr.ee/NicolaJaneUK

I'm a UK author, based in Nottinghamshire. I live with my husband of many years, our two teenage boys and our four little dogs. I write MC and Mafia romance with plenty of drama and chaos. I also love to read similar books. My favourite author is Tillie Cole. Before I became a full-time author, I was a teaching assistant working in a primary school.

If you'd like to follow my writing journey, join my readers group on Facebook, the link is above.

If you're a fabulous book blogger, then I need you! I'm not kidding—I really do need you to fill in the form below and join my blogging team. What you guys do is amazing and authors depend on you to get them out there. If you think you can help, then join using linktr.ee, above.

Other books in this series